W9-DEX-068

A Camel
Called April

DIANA HENDRY

A Camel
Called April

Illustrated by Thor Wickstrom

Lothrop, Lee & Shepard Books　　　New York

For Anne Kernighan

Text copyright © 1990 by Diana Hendry
Illustrations copyright © 1991 by Thor Wickstrom
First published in Great Britain by Julia MacRae Books, a division of Walker Books
Ltd.

First U.S. edition 1991 1 2 3 4 5 6 7 8 9 10

Library of Congress Cataloging in Publication Data
Hendry, Diana, A Camel called April / by Diana Hendry ; illustrated by Thor Wickstrom.
    p.   cm. Summary: When the animals in Harry's dreams settle in the park
across the street, the park gardener finds homes in the zoo for all of them, except
the stubborn camel. ISBN 0-688-10193-3 [1. Dreams—Fiction. 2. Parks—Fiction. 3. Camels—Fiction. 4. Animals—Fiction.] I. Wickstrom, Thor,
ill. II. Title.
PZ7.H38586Cam   1990 [Fic]—dc20
90-6371 CIP AC

Friendship is like the camel:
once started there is no way
of stopping it. — *Flaubert*

Chapter One

In the middle of the city was a square. Golden Square.

In the middle of the square was a park. Vagary Park.

Tall trees grew in the park and tall houses grew all around the square and in one of these houses lived Harold Arnold Percival Pemberton Yorick, otherwise known as Harry.

Harry was six. He lived at Number 12

Golden Square and from his bedroom window he had a very fine view of the park. He could see the curly-headed Scotch pine trees, the Lebanon cedar tree that was like a big, dark umbrella, and the tall poplar trees that were like giants' brooms. He could see the swings and the paddling pool and the hut where the park gardener kept his spades and rakes. He could see the fountain where the dogs liked to pause for a drink and the benches where the old people liked to sit and gossip. He could see the sloping avenues between the poplar trees where Jem Brewer, on his skateboard "Ratbones," and Charlie Piggot, on his skateboard "Gnash," went zigzagging home.

Harry was the sort of boy who asked "what if" a lot. What if there was a magic skateboard that could skate you from here to China in half a minute? What if the Scotch pines grew so tall they touched the clouds? What if the fountain fountained lemonade?

And Harry had amazing dreams. It rained jelly babies in Harry's dreams. Birds swam, fishes flew, and lollipops grew on trees in Harry's dreams. But the really strange dreams began that spring, just after Harry had had chicken pox.

Harry dreamed a lion. And when he woke up and looked out the window at the park—there it was, prowling about the jungle gym. On top of the jungle gym were four businessmen, one typist, and two nurses, who had been walking through the park on their way to work when the lion appeared.

There was a great hullabaloo in the

square. Police cars wailed their sirens. A
fire engine came wha-wha-wha-wha-wha-
wha-ing up the road. There were anxious
faces at every window and a police car
with a megaphone on its roof drove
round and round the square saying,
"PLEASE STAY IN YOUR HOUSES.
NOBODY IS TO COME OUTSIDE. A
LION HAS ESCAPED FROM THE ZOO.
PLEASE STAY IN YOUR HOUSES."

The park gardener climbed onto the
roof of his hut. Harry could see his legs
trembling.

Harry looked very carefully at the lion.
Of course it must have escaped from the
zoo. But what if . . . ? What if it hadn't
escaped from the zoo but from Harry's
dream?

Very soon four lion-keepers arrived
from the zoo. They threw the lion an

enormous hunk of meat and while he was eating it, the smallest lion-keeper crept up and gave the lion an injection in his bottom. The lion staggered a bit as if he were drunk and then fell down, fast asleep and snoring. The other lion-keepers wrapped him in a big net and carried him off to the van. Everyone cheered.

The four businessmen, one typist, and two nurses climbed down from the jungle gym and went off to work. The firemen had to help the gardener off the roof. Everything was quiet again in Vagary Park in Golden Square.

But the next night Harry dreamed a hippopotamus. And in the morning there it was, wallowing in the paddling pool and looking rather surprised. People were not so frightened of a

hippopotamus. A group of children on their way to school stood around the pool feeding the hippopotamus apples and cakes from their packed lunches.

The zoo men were there again—the hippopotamus-keepers this time. One of them was arguing with the gardener.

"This is very careless of you," said the gardener, "losing animals like this. First a lion. Now a hippopotamus."

"Now, look here," said the hippopotamus-keeper, with his hands on his hips. "This hippopotamus isn't our hippopotamus. We counted ours this morning. Both of them. And they are still there. We don't know where this hippopotamus came from and if you don't mend your manners we'll leave him here!"

They had to get a crane to winch the

hippopotamus into a big tank of water and then they had to winch the tank onto a truck.

The next night Harry dreamed of monkeys. And there they were in the morning, having a lovely time, swinging from poplar tree to poplar tree and climbing to the very top of the Scotch pines.

The people in Vagary Park were getting used to strange animals now. They looked out their windows and said, "Oh! It's monkeys this morning!" and carried on with their breakfasts.

The monkey-keepers from the zoo were very angry. The park gardener was very worried. Why did all these animals come to *his* park? The monkeys were hard to catch. The zoo men had to go to the baker and buy an enormous bag of

buns to tempt the monkeys down out of the trees.

Harry thought it was time he confessed.

The gardener and the zoo men were gazing up at the tallest pine tree when Harry arrived. Two monkeys were dropping pine cones on their heads.

"Excuse me," said Harry.

"We're very busy just now, lad," said the zoo man without looking at Harry. "We're trying to catch these 'ere monkeys."

"I'm afraid they're *my* monkeys," said Harry, turning very red.

The zoo man did look at Harry then. "No jokes, lad," he said. "What do you mean, they're *your* monkeys?"

"I dreamed them," said Harry.

"You dreamed them!" echoed the zoo

man, laughing and patting Harry's head.

"Yes," said Harry. "*And* I dreamed the lion and the hippopotamus."

"I wish I was dreaming," said the zoo man, digging into his bag for another bun. "Now, run along, lad. We've got work to do here."

Harry turned away unhappily. But the gardener stopped him. The gardener was a short, stocky man who smoked a pipe. He had gray-green eyes, the color of tree trunks. "You live over there, don't you?" he said, pointing to Harry's house.

"Yes," said Harry.

"I've seen you at the window and wondered why you weren't at school," said the gardener.

"I've had chicken pox," said Harry. "And I *did* dream those animals. Really I did."

"Well, maybe you did and maybe you didn't," said the gardener, "but off you go now while we catch the rest of these monkeys."

That night Harry dreamed a giraffe. There it was in the morning, nibbling the tops off the pine trees. This time the gardener didn't call for the zoo man. Instead he knocked on Harry's door.

"Yes," said Harry, "I know. There's a giraffe in the park. I dreamed him there last night."

"Look," said the gardener, puffing thoughtfully on his pipe, "I've got an idea. Do you think you could try and dream the giraffe back to where he came from?"

"I could try," said Harry doubtfully. "Where *do* giraffes come from?"

"Africa," said the gardener. "I've

brought you a book with pictures of
Africa in it. Look at it before you fall
asleep and see if you can dream this
giraffe back into Africa."

So that night Harry lay in bed with
pictures of the African bush and giraffes.
And it was quite easy! He dreamed of lots
of giraffes in a safari park and the dream
giraffe of Vagary Park lolloped off to join
them.

"There you are!" said the gardener the
next morning. "That's saved me a lot of
bother. But I'm a bit tired of animals
now. Do you think you could try
dreaming me some really fine roses or a
nice bed of delphiniums?"

"I'll try," said Harry. And when he
went to bed that night he took with him
a gardening book full of pictures of roses
and delphiniums.

But he didn't dream of roses and delphiniums.

Harry dreamed a camel.

Chapter Two

Ad there it was in the park the next morning. A rather beautiful camel with a single tufted hump, long, knobbly-kneed legs, long eyelashes, a soft and gentle mouth, and a stringy bit of a tail.

The camel liked it in the park. She liked the avenues between the poplar trees, the paddling pool, and the bar across the top of the swings because this

was a good place on which to scratch her itchy chin.

The gardener came rushing to Harry's door.

"Where're my roses?" he cried. "Where're my delphiniums? And why have I got a camel instead?"

"I'm terribly sorry," said Harry. "I did try to dream about roses and delphiniums but April just drifted in."

"April!" shrieked the gardener.

"That's her name," said Harry apologetically.

"Look," said the gardener, puffing deeply on his pipe, "do you think you could try and have a nap this morning, a quick forty winks perhaps, and dream this camel—this April—back again? Dream of the Sahara Desert. That's where camels live. Dream lots and lots of sand."

"I'll try," said Harry. But even though he curled up on his bed and snuggled his teddy, he didn't feel a bit sleepy. When he went over to the park to tell the gardener this, he found that April had fallen asleep underneath the Lebanon cedar and the gardener was sitting beside her, eating his sandwiches.

"I'm just not sleepy. I'll try tonight," said Harry. "A desert, you said?"

"Yes. The Sahara Desert," said the gardener, saving a few crusts for April. He had tethered her to the Lebanon cedar and quite a crowd of children had gathered round to look at her.

"Can we have a ride, please, mister?" asked one boy.

"This camel isn't for riding. It's just here on a visit. It's going back to the Sahara tonight," said the gardener.

"Wow! That's a long way!" said the boy.

"She's going by air," said the gardener loftily. "Tomorrow she'll just vanish—like a dream! You'll see!"

"Pity we can't have a ride," said the boy, and he wandered away.

That night Harry went to bed with a book about nomads and their camels traveling through the Sahara. Camels, he learned, were called ships of the desert.

And Harry *did* dream of April. In his dream April said, "I like your dream, Harry. Dreams are as big as deserts. I can wander about your dreams forever. I think I'll stay in your dreams at night and spend my days in the park."

"You can't do that!" said Harry (in his dream). "Camels don't belong in English dreams. They belong in African deserts."

"I don't care," said April. "I like it

here. We camels have very independent minds, you know. You can't just push us about." And with that the camel sat down. And although Harry prodded her and talked nicely to her and said how happy she would be as a ship of the desert, April would not budge.

When Harry woke up, he rushed to his window to look out, and there was April. She and the gardener were having breakfast together. The gardener was sitting on the In-Beloved-Memory-of-Mary-Loder bench and April stood behind him, nibbling his hair now and again and helping him out with his corn flakes.

Harry forgot his own breakfast and rushed over to the park.

"Hello," said the gardener. "What happened to your dream of the Sahara?"

"I did dream a desert," said Harry,

sitting down beside him on the bench, "but April wouldn't go. She said my dream was as big as a desert, only more fun, and she was going to stay."

April bent down her long, snaky neck at this and tried nibbling a piece of Harry's hair. She didn't like it.

"I'm not really surprised," said the gardener. "Camels are famous for being very stubborn. Sometimes the nomads have to light fires underneath them to get them to move on."

"I wouldn't like to do that," said Harry, "not even in a dream."

At this point April, who had been chewing a piece of poplar tree and turning it round and round in her mouth, spat.

"That's something else camels are famous for," said the gardener happily. "Spitting."

30

"Well, what are we going to do?" asked Harry. "Are you going to call the zoo?"

The gardener stroked April's nose.

"No, not this time," he said. "The truth is I've taken rather a shine to April. A man needs something that's a bit dreamlike in his life, something a bit strange and not-quite-of-this-world."

April batted her long eyelashes at both of them.

"I was thinking I'd keep her," said the gardener. "In fact, sitting here on the Beloved Memory bench, I thought to myself—what if I built a camel house next to my hut?"

"What a wonderful idea!" said Harry.

But just at that moment a very large gentleman with a fat, important stomach came striding across the park. He was wearing a bowler hat and carrying an umbrella. Behind him was a policeman.

"Excuse me," said the fat gentleman. "My name is Fred Knobbs and I am chairman of the Parks Committee. It has come to my attention that you are keeping a camel in the park. This is not allowed. That camel will have to go." And Mr. Knobbs pointed his umbrella at April.

April bent down her snaky neck and very gently removed Mr. Knobbs's bowler hat.

Chapter Three

It doesn't say anything in the park rules about not allowing camels," said the gardener. He pointed to a board at the entrance to the park. The rules were very old. The gardener read them aloud.

1. No person shall stand, sit, lie upon, or walk over any flower bed.
2. No person shall play or take part in any game except on the space allotted therefor.

3. No person shall at any time drive
or bring into the park any horse,
donkey, cattle, sheep, or pig.

"There you are," said the gardener,
"nothing about camels." (I'm very glad I
didn't dream a pig, thought Harry.)

Mr. Knobbs waved his umbrella angrily
at the park rules. "Well, of course it
doesn't mention camels," he cried.
"Camels aren't English, are they? When
those rules were made, nobody thought
of camels. But if they had, they would
have been on the list. In fact, I shall see
to it that they are added to the list.
Tomorrow."

"Actually," said Harry, "this camel isn't
a real camel. It's a dream camel."

Mr. Knobbs glared at Harry. "Now, boy,"
he said, puffing up his stomach and
looking more important than ever, "you
can't make a fool out of me, you know. I

am chairman of the Parks Committee. That is a Very Important Position. If that was a dream camel, then I would be asleep. And I'm not." Mr. Knobbs pinched himself just to make sure. And then he pinched Harry because he felt so cross.

April looked at Mr. Knobbs with her large eyes. She flapped her eyelashes a couple of times and then spat on Mr. Knobbs's left shoe. Mr. Knobbs went very red.

"Now, now," said the gardener, taking long, soothing puffs on his pipe, "why don't we all sit down and talk this over?"

They all sat down on the In-Beloved-Memory-of-Mary-Loder bench. It seemed to make everyone calmer. April wandered off and lay down under the umbrella of the Lebanon cedar.

"I was wondering," said the gardener,

36

IN LOVING
MEMORY
OF
MARY LODE

speaking very slowly in between puffs on his pipe, "what if we put April—I mean the camel—to work? What if she made some money for Vagary Park—for all the parks?"

Mr. Knobbs folded his hands over his stomach and laughed. "Dream money, I suppose," he said.

"Well, no," said the gardener. "What I was thinking of was this. What if we kept the camel in the park and allowed people to have rides on her back? We could charge 20 pence a ride. They don't have a camel at the zoo. I'm sure people would come a long way to see a camel in a park."

"We could become the most famous park in England!" said Harry excitedly.

"Ummm!" said Mr. Knobbs slowly and thoughtfully. "Ummm! The most famous park in England, eh?"

"Well, yes," said the gardener. "And I expect a parks committee that thought up such an idea would be quite famous too."

"They'd probably want to interview you on television," said Harry.

"On television, eh?" said Mr. Knobbs, smiling. "Me and the camel side by side. Both of us smiling."

"Yes," said Harry and the gardener together.

"She mustn't spit, though," said Mr. Knobbs anxiously.

"Oh no!" said the gardener. "We'd arrange that. You see, she's not park trained yet. But I'll have a word with her about spitting."

"I shall go and arrange an Extraordinary General Meeting of the Parks Committee," said Mr. Knobbs, standing up. "You will be hearing from me shortly." And he marched away, swinging his umbrella very happily.

Harry and the gardener did a little dance together round and round the fountain. April watched them. She thought dancing was very silly.

Chapter Four

Two days later a letter arrived at the gardener's hut. This is what it said.

Dear Gardener and Harry,

We had a very long Committee
Meeting about your camel, April.
We have decided that we would
like April to stay in Vagary Park
and to become Camel-in-Residence.
She will give the children rides
during the summer and you can
build a camel house next to the
hut. The Committee would like to
have a party in the park so that
April can be made properly
welcome.

Yours greenly,

B. Knobbs

B. Knobbs, Chairman
P.S. We think it should be 30p a
ride.

Harry and the gardener had another dance round the fountain.

"You can stay, April!" said Harry, giving the camel a big hug. April closed one eye and winked.

The Parks Committee arranged a big party to welcome April as Camel-in-Residence of Vagary Park. All the committee came, and all the people who lived in Golden Square. Jem Brewer came on "Ratbones" and Charlie Piggot came on "Gnash." A special saddle had been made for April. It had brightly colored leather tassels and on either side of it were three wooden seats so that April could carry six children at once. It was called a howdah. "Now she's a ship of the park," said Harry.

At the party the children were given free rides. Harry and the gardener walked about looking very proud (but not quite as proud as Mr. Knobbs, who

was given the first ride on the camel and photographed wearing his special gold chain so that everyone would know he was chairman of the Parks Committee).

April settled down very happily at Vagary Park. She liked to follow the gardener about while he was digging the flower beds or mowing the lawns. She became very friendly with the park regulars and they became very fond of her.

The gardener built her a tall house next to his hut, and she used it when the weather was bad. But she didn't need it at night because then she drifted off, on her long, knobbly-kneed legs, into Harry's dreams.

Harry didn't always see her in his dreams. There were some nights when he knew that April was there—but she was asleep in a corner of his dream.

Those dreams were like plays in which April didn't have a part. On some nights, when April was feeling homesick for the desert, she and Harry would dream themselves into the Sahara and Harry would ride on her back over miles and miles of sand. Sometimes April would interrupt a dream when she found it boring.

So many children wanted a ride on April's back that the Parks Committee made a lot of money and they bought new roses and delphiniums and swings for parks that didn't have any swings.

The rules on the board at the entrance to the park were changed. Rule number three now said this:

> No person shall at any time drive or bring into the park any horse, donkey, cattle, sheep, or pig. But a camel is all right.

In the middle of the city was a square called Golden Square. In the middle of the square was a park called Vagary Park. In the middle of the park was a camel called April.

Everyone needs something a bit dreamlike in life," says Diana Hendry. "Something a bit strange and not-quite-of-this-world." One of her own dreams was of a camel. When she woke, she couldn't get that camel out of her head. She began to think what fun it would be if a camel, a dream camel—*her* camel—came to live in the park near her home.

Thor Wickstrom, like Harry, has spent a lot of time dreaming animals into reality. He says he likes Harry and his dreams because they mess up everybody's routine: "It's something every child—and every artist—enjoys watching."

A Camel called April and *The Not-Anywhere House,* both illustrated by Mr. Wickstrom, are among Ms. Hendry's first books to be published in the United States. She lives in Bristol, England, and he lives in Pine Plains, New York.